D1353685

The Naughty Fairy's

NAUGHTY SURPRISE

The Naughtiest Fairy's Naughty Surprise
First published in 2006
by Meadowside Children's Books
185 Fleet Street, London, EC4A 2HS
Text and illustrations © Nick Ward 2006

The right of Nick Ward to be identified as the
author and illustrator of this work has been
asserted by him in accordance with the Copyright,
Designs and Patents Act, 1988

A CIP catalogue record for this book
is available from the British Library
Printed in China

ISBN 10 pbk 1-84539-210-8
ISBN 13 pbk 978-1-84539-210-9

ISBN 10 hbk 1-84539-211-6
ISBN 13 hbk 978-1-84539-211-6

10 9 8 7 6 5 4 3 2

The Naughty Fairy's

NAUGHTY SURPRISE

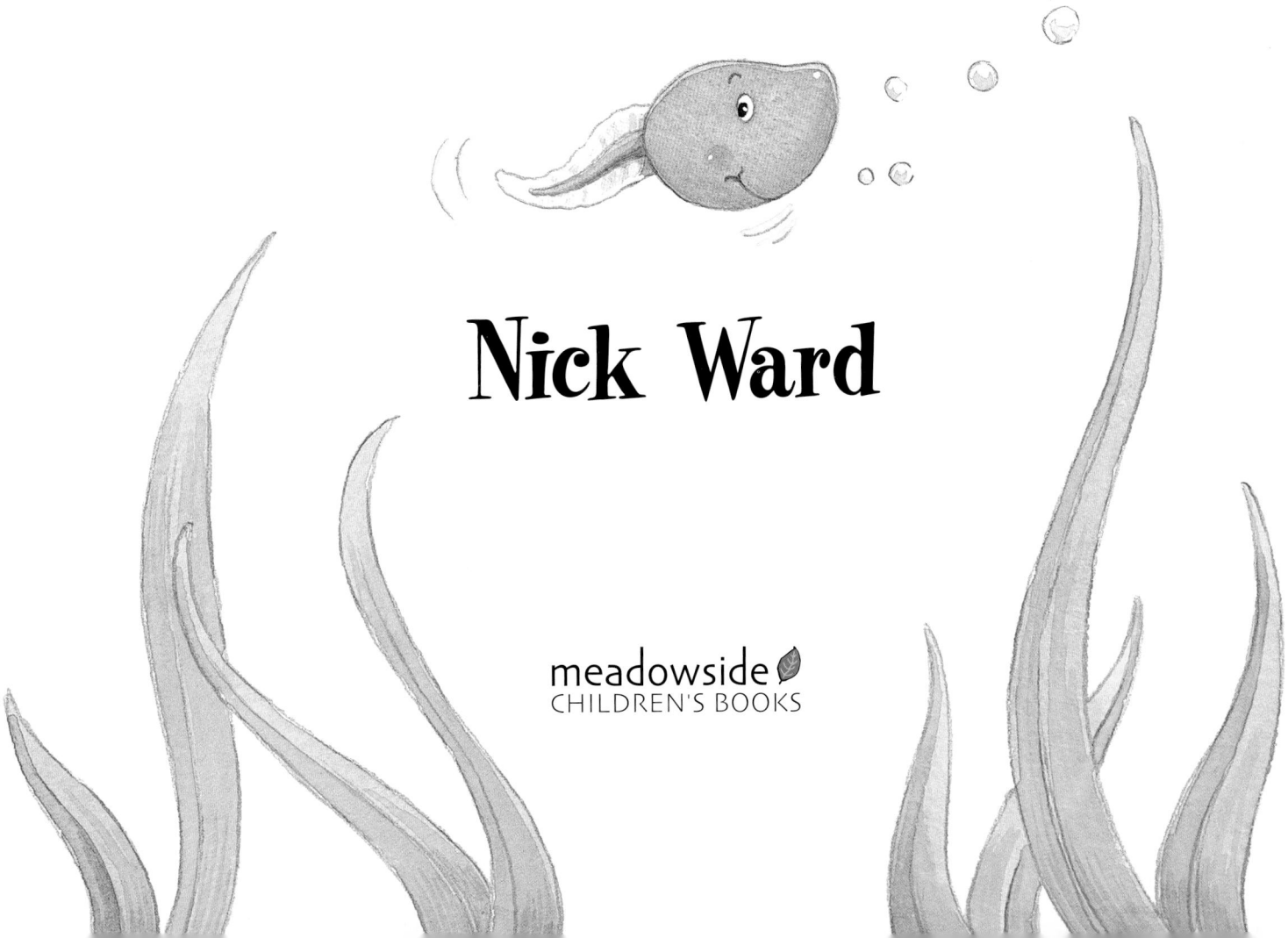

Nick Ward

meadowside
CHILDREN'S BOOKS

In a quiet corner
of the palace gardens,
deep in a still green pond,
a little tadpole popped
out of his egg...

"Wow!"
he gasped
as he saw all the wonderful
creatures swimming around him.

"What will I be
when I grow up?"

"What will I be when I grow up?" he asked
a wise old fish. "Will I be as big and brave as you?"

"What's the hurry?" smiled the wise old fish.
"Anything may happen. Just wait and see!"

So the impatient little tadpole
waited ...

and waited ...

until one day...

"Well, who would have guessed!" croaked the little frog, jumping onto a lily-pad. "I'm a fr-"

But just then a passing princess
scooped him up.
"Are you my handsome prince?"
she asked, giving him a kiss.

"Oh dear,"
said the little
frog, feeling
another change
coming on...

"I'm a handsome prince!" he cried, and was just about to give the princess another kiss, when...

WHOOOSH!

A naughty fairy grabbed the princess and whisked her away to a tall rickety tower.

"Help!" she cried. "Save me!"

So the handsome prince ran through the woods and over a mountain, till he came to the tall rickety tower. But two ugly trolls were guarding the tower.

"Gnarr!" they roared, scrunching up their faces.

"That's not scary," said the handsome prince.

And he pulled such horrible faces that the trolls screamed and ran away!

So the handsome prince rescued the princess, which turned him into a...

Hero! "You're my hero!" sighed the princess, and the hero quickly marched the Big Bad Wolf and some big bully giants out of town.

(That was a hero's job, you see.)

"And don't come back till you're sorry!" he ordered.

The princess was so grateful to him for making her country safe that she decided to marry her hero. And this turned him into a rich and powerful...

Daddy! "Yippee, I'm a daddy!"
He was so excited that he held a huge party.

Everyone was invited:
the Three Bears,

the Three Little Pigs and

Little Red Riding Hood.

Everyone except the naughty fairy!

The naughty fairy was so annoyed that she wrapped a naughty magic spell in a box, and tied a beautiful bow on top. "I'll teach him!" she grumbled.

The naughty fairy put on a disguise
and took her present to the king...

"Congratulations!" she cackled.
But the king recognized the fairy
and guessed it was a trick.

"I can't undo the bow," he pretended.
"Oh, give it here, silly!" said the naughty fairy.

And she ripped off the paper and opened the box.

"Oh no!"

The magic spell whizzed around the fairy's head and - POP! she disappeared.

"Where has she gone?" cried the king.

In a quiet corner of the palace gardens, deep in a still green pond, a naughty little tadpole gasped at all the wonderful creatures.
POP!
"What will I be when I grow up?"
she wondered...

For Peter and Hazel.

Beware of Naughty Fairies!

N.W.